I0796656

Tyrannosaurus Rex
Maria Koran
EYEDISCOVER

Go to **www.eyediscover.com** and enter this book's unique code.

BOOK CODE

AVZ77356

EYEDISCOVER brings you optic readalongs that support active learning.

Published by AV² by Weigl
350 5th Avenue, 59th Floor New York, NY 10118
Website: www.eyediscover.com

Library of Congress Control Number: 2019945848

ISBN 978-1-7911-0764-2 (hardcover)

Printed in Guangzhou, China
1 2 3 4 5 6 7 8 9 0 23 22 21 20 19

072019
121818

Project Coordinator: John Willis
Designer: Mandy Christiansen and Ana María Vidal

All illustrations by Jon Hughes, pixel-shack.com.
Weigl acknowledges Alamy, Dreamstime, iStock, and Shutterstock as the primary image suppliers for this title.

EYEDISCOVER provides enriched content, optimized for tablet use, that supplements and complements this book. EYEDISCOVER books strive to create inspired learning and engage young minds in a total learning experience.

Watch
Video content brings each page to life.

Browse
Thumbnails make navigation simple.

Read
Follow along with text on the screen.

Listen
Hear each page read aloud.

Your EYEDISCOVER Optic Readalongs come alive with...

Audio
Listen to the entire book read aloud.

Video
High resolution videos turn each spread into an optic readalong.

OPTIMIZED FOR

- TABLETS
- WHITEBOARDS
- COMPUTERS
- AND MUCH MORE!

Tyrannosaurus Rex

In this book, you will learn about

- what it looked like
- what it ate
- where it lived

and much more!

Tyrannosaurus Rex is called "King of the Dinosaurs." It is also known as T. rex.

T. rex is one of the fiercest and biggest dinosaurs that ever lived.

T. rex was a carnivore, or meat eater. It was an excellent hunter.

It had the strongest bite of any known land animal. There were 60 long, sharp teeth in its mouth.

T. rex walked on two legs. Its tail helped it balance.

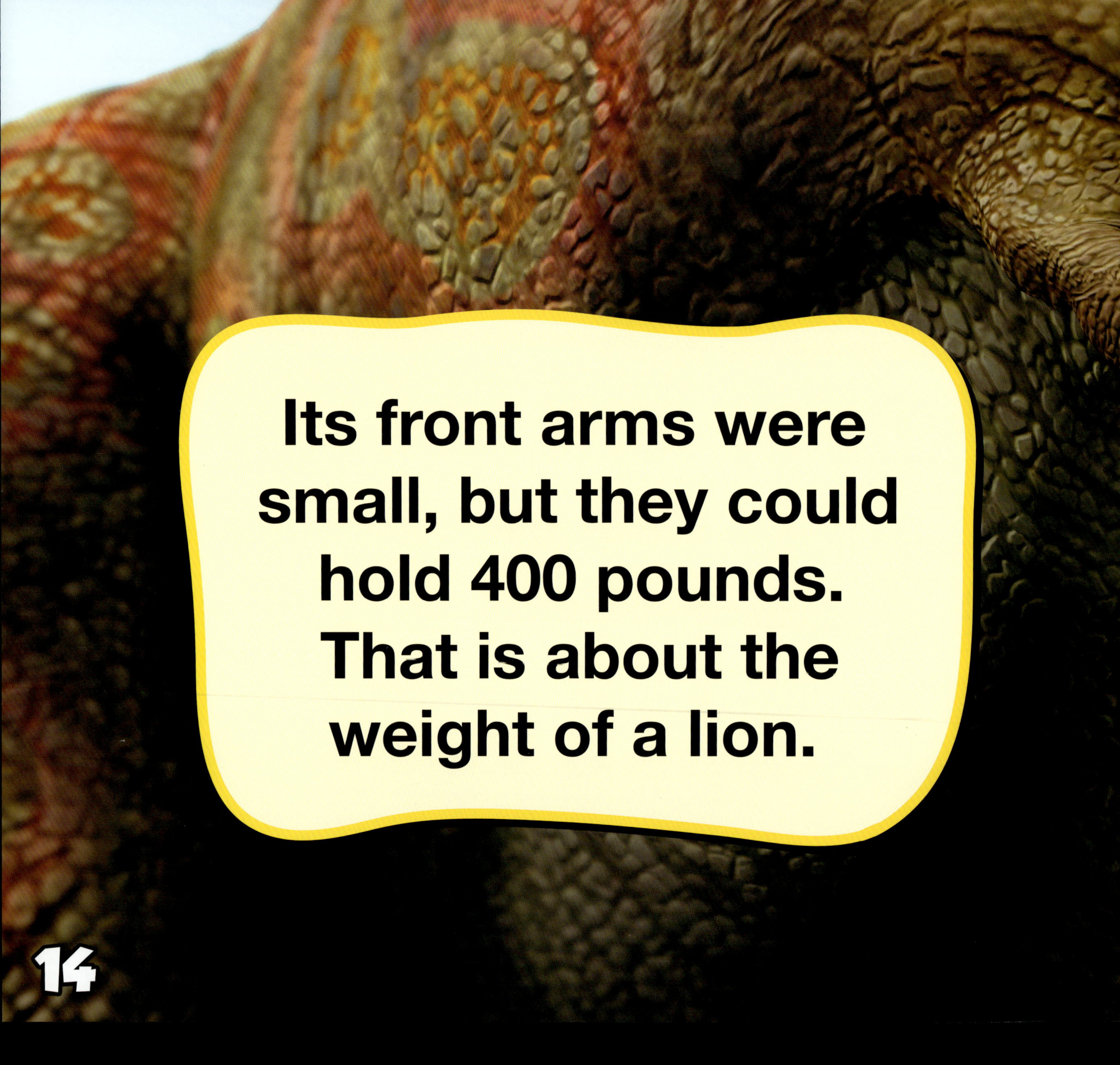

Its front arms were small, but they could hold 400 pounds. That is about the weight of a lion.

T. rex lived for about 30 years.

It lived near rivers and swamps across North America.

You can see fossils of T. rex in museums. The best preserved T. rex is at the Field Museum in Chicago.

TYRANNOSAURUS REX BY THE NUMBERS

T. rex could **eat** up to **500 pounds** of meat in **one bite**. (227 kilograms)

T. rex was about **three times** the length of a crocodile. It could be up to **46 feet long**. (14 meters)

T. rex was **heavily muscled** and weighed up to **15,000 pounds**. (6,800 kg)

With a **jaw** that was **4 feet** long, T. rex had **a bite** strong enough **to tear** through the roof of a car. (1.2 m)

The **first** **T. rex** fossil was discovered more than **115 years** ago.

KEY WORDS

Research has shown that as much as 65 percent of all written material published in English is made up of 300 words. These 300 words cannot be taught using pictures or learned by sounding them out. They must be recognized by sight. This book contains 40 common sight words to help young readers improve their reading fluency and comprehension. This book also teaches young readers several important content words, such as proper nouns. These words are paired with pictures to aid in learning and improve understanding.

Page	Sight Words First Appearance
4	also, as, is, it, of, the
7	and, ever, one, that
8	a, an, or, was
11	animal, any, had, in, its, land, long, there, were
13	on, two, walked
14	about, but, could, small, they
17	for, years
18	America, near, rivers
21	at, can, see, you

Page	Content Words First Appearance
4	dinosaurs, king, T. rex, Tyrannosaurus Rex
8	carnivore, hunter, meat eater
11	bite, mouth, teeth
13	legs, tail
14	arms, lion, pounds, weight
18	North America, swamps
21	Chicago, Field Museum, fossils, museums

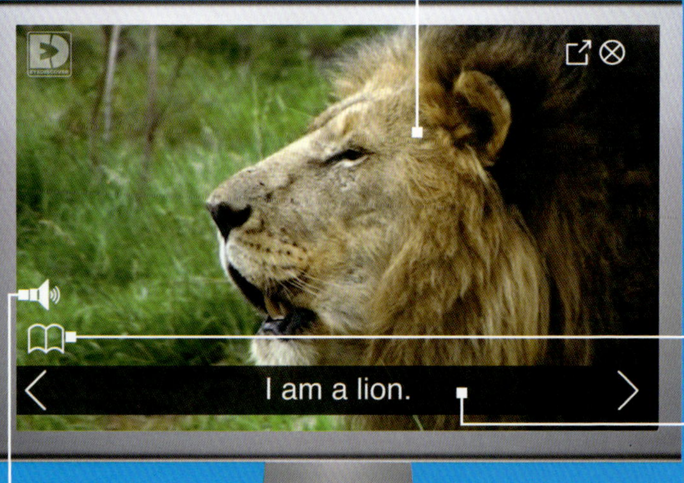

Watch
Video content brings each page to life.

Browse
Thumbnails make navigation simple.

Read
Follow along with text on the screen.

Listen
Hear each page read aloud.

Go to www.eyediscover.com and enter this book's unique code.

BOOK CODE

AVZ77356